BEGINNINGS
Selected Prose Poetry

By
Benbo Smith

Foreword by
Miles Wall

A Splashlime publication

BEGINNINGS
Selected Prose Poetry

First published in Great Britain by Splashlime, an imprint of Splashlime Ltd.

www.splashlime.com

First Print Edition May, 2017 - ISBN 978-0-9956179-0-2 (This Book).

First Ebook Edition March, 2016 - ISBN 978-1-5262-0180-5

A CIP catalogue record for this ebook is available from the British Library.

Dedication

For Sophie, Gordon, Clare, and Richard. Who always believe in me. The daft sods.

And for:

Cath of Newcastle, Gabi of Berlin, Norm of Belfast, Ri of Berlin, and Bryan of London. Who are always in my thoughts.

Europa's Neu Leitmotíf, dedicated to Alan Kurdî, who should not have died so young.

Foreword by Miles Wall

Smith's poems deal with real life, the grim, the hard, the political and social economics of constraint. His poetry is a platform for invoking discussion with the reader. He firmly believes that a poem can have its own and distinct voice, sending a message to the reader that provokes a response.

I will tell you now that Smith is not always an easy author to read. His prose is poetic, yet not prose poetry. His free verse style sometimes follows established rules of meter and form just when you have realised that it does not. He will break rhymes with no warning, and start a poem with prose, only to switch into verse halfway through. Yes, Smith is hard to read. Yet with hard work, you will see under the surface of this quasi accessible text, and when you do, it will have been worth it.

Smith will often help, for he is aware that his eclectic use of styles can present barriers to the reader. In his short poetic narrative "Judgement", Smith makes a point of using a Germanic word, phonically spelled in English so that the non-German reader can pronounce the word with the intended sound. Thus he uses "toad" instead of "Tod". In doing so he takes a risk. It is easy to imagine that the reader may infer a Germanic royal amphibian, probably hailing from the Schloß Neuschwanstein. German speakers among you may now be jumping up and down asking "Where for out is our tea?"

It is clear that the time Smith spent living and working in Canada, and the United States in his formative years reflects in his outlook. In the poem "A Continent of Nations" a discoloured thread of adventure can be related through his reference to the early explorers Lewis and Clark, reflecting the eventual loss of the native peoples' land to the march of European progress.

In "Pioneer Jacks", the train, which features as a meter, a rare nod to convention from Smith, holds a genetic ident. His grandfather worked his way west from Nova Scotia to Vancouver as a lumberjack, and travelled across the continent on the Canadian Pacific Railway returning to the UK when the great depression hit. His mother's arrival in Canada was captured on the front page of Maclean's, as Canada imported British secretaries in the 1960s; she also returned to the UK.

Smith himself, the third generation of the family to live and work in Canada, spent a year in Vancouver and fell in love with the mountains, space, and raw excitement of a city on the edge. His poem "Searching the New World" is an introspection on the hunt for himself one night in British Columbia.

Visits to the South of France have also had an impact on his work. There is a reference in "Côte d'Azur"; the part-line, "the clarity of the azure carpet of my perspective", is a reference to the azure coloured sea from which the area gets its name. As always with Smith, there is also a second meaning to this phrase. See if you can decipher it, you will need to read the line in context.

Smith's work is full of literary symbolism. For example in "Europa's Neu Leitmotif" he references Wagner and Shakespeare within just a few lines of each other to discuss European migration and refugees from the middle east in contemporary times. In order not to spoil your enjoyment I will not disclose the references here, but allow you to discover them for yourself.

I hope that you will persevere with Smith, as I have. I promise much joy will come of your labours.

Miles Wall, London, February 2016.

With Healthy Alert

"The poet who writes 'free' verse is like Robinson Crusoe on his desert island: he must do all his cooking, laundry and darning for himself. In a few exceptional cases, this manly independence produces something original and impressive, but more often the result is squalor - dirty sheets on the unmade bed and empty bottles on the unswept floor."

W. H. Auden - "Writing" in The Dyer's Hand, and Other Essays (1962).

Côte d'Azur

I wake in a small hotel room, with a city view. A noise on the street below has awoken me two hours before due. In mourning for lost sleep, I open the window and see before me, myself in the reflection of the church window across the street.

I take stock of the balding fat man I see, as if it is not really me. I say to myself, "Hey, are you going to Èze for the walk?", Of course, I could not talk. I close the French shutters, and clamber back into bed.

Up now for real and dressing in a hurry, I scurry out of the hotel to catch the sunshine bus, full of rust. The terminus is noisy, and not at all glamorous. The derrière of Nice, and smelling of diesel.

The bus is late, the french gesticulate. I shrug my shoulders, for no difference will it make, I'm already late. At last, it comes, and we all aboard. Myself and the shopping nuns.

The bus rounds the port where empty boats are waiting to take the glitterati aboard. Then up the hill to the moyenne corniche. Along the coast, with villas to boast.

The noise of the city behind us, the Alps on our left, with the sea below à la droite. Over a bridge that traverses a gorge and into view my destination. Èze, a high top medieval on the edge of France, my heart makes a little dance.

I climb down from the bus, it leaves at once. Alone for a moment, the world stops.

Tranquillity descends over me, as the mist falls from mountains above. A priest walks past with withered gait, I should not hesitate I will be late.

It's early, and the tourists have not arrived, nor has the warming sun, as I chill in the shadows of the mountain, I think of the ashes I must spread. For my passenger is long dead.

I search for the trailhead as I start my walk. It's tucked in beside the entrance to a hotel with valueless sculpture gardens. Gaudy and not an ideal position, next to a medieval vision.

I bounce as I walk down the slope, but it's ok I can cope. The river we crossed on the bus above, in the gorge now accompanies me. It's the mid summer and the water's rhythm is in tempo with me.

I have found it now, the lookout post, where the dead wants it most. For here where Nietzsche did walk and did not talk, my passenger wants his final rest.

It's noon on the spot. I pull from my sack a darkened jar, and toss myself just so far. The world stops.

I have been walking all day long, and now I have reached the bay at the foot of the mountain. Secluded on three sides with a wooden pier to swim to, just past the jelly fish and jagged rocks.

On Noël's[1] Cap I did stare back at Nietzsche's[2] trail across the clarity of the azure carpet of my perspective, and reflected with the sweet fragonardian ezescent.

The sun has lowered to the mystic hour. In solitude, the Neptune pool is mine, and I swim naked to enjoy. The water washes my nectar away, and now the mountain starts to cry.

---

[1] Noël's Cap refers to the house that Noël Coward lived in on Cap Ferrat, a short distance from Èze-sur-Mer.

[2] The steep and winding trail from Èze to Èze-sur-Mer is named after the German philosopher Nietzsche, who used to enjoy its breath taking views over the Mediterranean.

Fabric of Man

He looked at the cobbled stone, dislodged and laying at the side of the pavement. It was a trapezoid, larger at the bottom than at the top. Both ends were finished in a way that you could expect them to form the platform on which one walks.

Why was this? Then he saw it. Each stone was the same, but by turning it over it interlocked with its neighbour to form a strong bond on which man could walk.

All stones were created equally, but some supported others more greatly to allow them to perform the fabric's function more efficiently.

And so it would be in life, each man born the same, kneeling on the labours of others to deliver the benefit to all. Man, the fabric, were all part of the same.

The stone cried, for his cousin is his brother, and his brother is his father, and his father is his mother. Packed tight and not free, this stone cried for me. Wrenched from his bedrock light now shed. His sister is chipped and slagged away. For this he must pay.

Weathered by rain his skin shines and hides his pain. There are stones from all over, some black, some grey, some pink and some green. All together, none the same, but all made and shaped by man in to a uniform existence, one up, one down, as together they stand.

Once a stone did depart, that hollowed out our heart. The dirt came in and so did the grass, it kicked us up the ass. Our fabric did tear and no one did care, we fell into disrepair. A new stone was made that was slicker than us, bonded firm without any fuss.

With no room to breathe this new stone smothered the land. The water had nowhere to go, and man did complain, when the flood came again. This time no ark, and man was now dark.

We were better made from different rock, it was the strength that heals. Now there is no diversity left, it's just a great homogeneous mess. Perhaps there is hope within our stone, if we look inside we can not hide, the colours in all of us kin shine out from within.

Judgement

Should I bend to the subtleties of class, or take morse coded routings of valour around the snake?

I watched as he perceived me over time. Looking for placement in stature of self. Constantly looking to judge, hoping to come out on top.

Where would the pendulum fixate. Should I pronounce an intervention to sway my fate?

Born equal under prophecy of the political. Balance tipped by opportunity afforded souls intertwined by nationhood of the democratic farce.

I longed for the far off confederacy in distant past. The uniting cast. Scorned by legacy of Orwellian reporting subjecting idealistic hope to rigours of just cause.

To the German toad I must advance, to precise the source. For I will both lower and rise with the tide of my ability independent, to serve my brother and not his.

Europa's Neu Leitmotif[1]

We are the underclass, the unwashed, the never to be mentioned. For all our knowledge and strength, you allow us to be down-trodden. We seek the route to our salvation, but 'tis blocked at every nation. A passage of humanity not open to us, by those unwilling hosts that play games of willkommen.[2]

We do not seek to exist this way, but this way we are. Massed in ranks of destitution, we the uncomfortable farce. The game is played again with every quadratic generation. Ejected from our ideal by the zeitleidenland[3] annexation. Nächste[4] Station, Nächste Station, Nächste Station.

Will's More pleaded for us, Rheinmädchens[5] do greet us. For we are your neu[6] river rock. To repay the substance of the forged ring we will. So that Europa may at last verse a humanitarian bill.

When will we hear a uniting cheer, from this the divided light of Saturn's pull? Seeking nations' craters in the tide of inhumanity, Oh cheer us free and take a step for thy dignity. Arrived have we, thus you see the mountain of us.

---

[1] "Leitmotif" German: operatic construct associated with Wagner. A tune or a musical theme, usually short in duration that is associated with a character, object or place.

[2] "willkommen" German: Welcome.

[3] "zeitleidenland" German: Time suffering country. A country that is suffering in hard times.

[4] "Nächste Station" German: Next station.

[5] "Rheinmädchens" German, from Wagner: Maidens of the river Rhine.

[6] "neu" German: New.

Night Shift

Arrive at scene after blueing the night. Men and children in fright. Car upended, body suspended. Racing pulse of the rescue driver, prompt action of the fire crew.

Forces gather to pump and sweat. Last corner taken too fast, now strangers regret. Young boy staring up from the concrete. His chest pumped by ambulance crew, alas he did not renew. Oh why did he not slow down, now the police frown.

Next morning as it is dawning, a new shout to an old lout. 78 yesterday, indigestion not got away. Jokes and checks, then the worst. The old boy croaks as the fire stokes. Onto the chest, in with the mask, oxygen on high, please God let this one last. Pulse checked, no rhythm.

Cannula, miraculous drugs inserted, shock delivered. Pulseless and still, hope fading, morning sun rising. Shocked wife and family, still we are pumping my crew mate and me. Breathing for him, the head bearer pauses, another shock and…

Ray of light peeps through the curtains from the night. Pulse returns, crew in shock, this one beat the clock. Transport arranged, light heartedness refrain. He will be alright, this old Jack.

Home to bed, neighbours waking, Thoughts of the dead, eyes not sinking. Partner awakes, "Good shift?", "Not bad, one all, it a shame Mort scored." Still thinking, not sleeping, wish I could go drinking.

The Highlanders

Hot breath in cold glen air, rising from damp nostrils that flair. Situated on the mound, the stag greets the dawning. A low roar of his vibrations calling. Rounding his hinds as they climb the steep side. The cold mist of morning, now parting with heather adorning.

Master and gillie breakfast hardened, stand fast in the hunting garden. Last day of season stalking, gear all reporting. Leaving the strath[1], passing the bothan[2], piece[3] in their poke[4], they laugh and joke.

Past the tree line now, mist moving, sun gleaming. As day noons with hinds at rest at last the stag can digest. His labours rewarded with pastures of heaven, old rusks and tusks with heather a must.

Gillie leading, master following, now glassing the hill. Searching the far slope, hoping to scope. Then on the crest a dark red breast. Antlers directing hind legs a massing. Between them the glen and damp watered hill.

Up high on exposed plateau, the cold is taking its toll. The wind is whispering, "get walking", "get walking". Overcast now, the wind is up, as the afternoon ages, the strynd[5] calls.

Tracking the stag breeze in face, our master and gillie, turn across burn and gully. Now discussing with hands and waves, they cut their journey through the indigenous carpet of the knitted scarf.

Smirr[6] now, down they go, shelter seeking. A change in wind, comfort as darkness calls. For facing into the storm, the smell of water draws. Towards the sheltered glen the clan prevail, down into the deepest of the vale.

Day noons, and legs wabbit[7] from the stalking, both men at rest in gully, talking.

Danger now on the breeze, the stag steels himself from his ease. "Humans" the wind is warning. Now terror is dawning.

Sherlock hat periscopes ditch; ranges stag they aim to bag. Rifle readied in silence; the well-oiled team prepare for the thrill, and sclim[8] the hill. Crawling forwards inching moors, stalking on all fours.

A crack of thunder and his world hurts. Gravity becomes heavy, ground a rushing, head a gushing. Pounding heart, legs fail to start, pain subsiding, life reminding. A buzzing silence, as dark adorning, mist reforming.

Crosshairs aligned and crack. The sport is won, the beast is done. Now they move over as hinds run. Master in delight, gillie grateful, for his work is done. The wind roars with dismay. Mack-a-shaw[9] now the nicht[10] is near, all done for another year.

---

[1] "strath" Scottish: A river valley that is wide and shallow.

[2] "bothan" Scottish: A hut.

[3] "piece" Scottish: A sandwich or packed lunch.

[4] "poke" Scottish: A small bag used for food.

[5] "strynd" Scottish: Descent.

[6] "smirr" Scottish: Fine rain, drizzle.

[7] "wabbit" Scottish: Exhausted or weak.

[8] "sclim" Scottish: Climb.

[9] "mack-a-shaw" Scottish: To get moving quickly.

[10] "nicht" Scottish: Night.

Life in Green C#

Perhaps we listen in green for that vibrant clarity before falling into ourselves.

Perhaps the sand in our dissatisfaction of progress is glass from our soul.

Perhaps the morning will bring comfort of a new spring, and hope will be reborn to a new beat.

Pioneer Jacks

On skid row all was quiet, as the moose made his way through the small timber town. The chasers were sleeping, the choker setters were sleeping, and the fallers were sleeping. In the valley below the great iron road was humming, for the first morning train was coming.

And in the boarding house the lifting men were sleeping, and in the brothel the noble men were sleeping, and above the supply store the Smith men were sleeping.

Only you were watching, while the brown bear passed the post hut, and the owl flew from under the station clock tower, soon now the waking hour.

And by the river in an old barn, the river hogs were sleeping, and the catty-men were sleeping. And in the tool shed the whistle punk slept next to his old donkey.

Now the foreman's wife has woken and has begun the breakfast, she has pride in her husband, but none in their son the bootlegger. And now the brave bearded suspender wearing, caulk boot wearing, heavy shirt wearing men are waking, and the day has begun.

Streams of men are converging on the mountain road, some from the town, and some from the camp higher up the hill. Then the iron shudders as the railroad ties take the weight of the huff and puff. The tie hacks with their broadaxes have made these lines tough.

Work has begun at the landing zone in the hills above. The chasers drag yesterday's detritus away, if only their horses could steady, they could be done already, and the steam donkey is waking up.

Up higher still the fallers and buckers pull their crosscut saw, and chop with their axe. "Timber….." and five tons fall to the floor. Choker setters run in, pulleys and rigging are set a jigging, and soon the big wheel pulled by the two old horses will pull the logs with the skidders to the watery shoot.

Down and down the logs go with ease in the flume amongst the trees, and now the train comes to a stop delivering the next crop of jacks and assorted hacks.

The skidders slide the logs off from the flume, expectant river hogs in their corks and spikes look forward to the rolling, and the river dance that afternoon.

The workers break backs as the nation grows richer, but a great economic storm is coming, and soon people will be running. But for now they still toil, with their axes, and ropes, and iron climbing hooks.

The river is filling with logs and catty-men, dancing for their supper. The train whistles, and the whistle punk whistles as if in reply. Now the train is leaving, pushing west again.

Up at the landing zone, the men are yelling and the steam donkey splutters, for the yarder did not hear the whistle punk alert, and now a new man lies still. The yarder is staring, standing motionless. One less Jack is heading home to Jill. Success is measured in timber produced and lives spared, today only the money men will prosper from the hill.

The sawmill downstream is waiting for the logs to arrive, but a jam in the river has put pay to today. The key log is still stuck and the water hogs call for the powder monkey to do his duty.

As the train passes the mill, its whistle is obscured by the explosion to set the logs in motion, as the splinters fall still. The lumber truck driver jumps, for he has been seen with the bootlegger at the base of the hill.

The iron road stops humming as the train pushes on, the evening is shadowing the town, and soon the men will return from the hill, and the brothel will awake, and the boarding house will serve chow.

Dark again now, but not all are still. There's a truck leaving town, for it's headed to a new camp further from the hill. This transient existence of the men's men and their lumber is moving yet again.

Now the train brings the next generation to sweat blood and sacrifice, these noble men, mighty men, lifting men, timber men, building the nation.

Tired Life Retired

So tired, ever tired. Tired of life, tired of the pain of reality. Tired of mundanity. So tired.

Change tired, change pain. Move focus, drive forward again. But so tired. Too tired.

Flowing in discordant streams of mildew. Gone the epiphany effervescence of the younger. So tired.

Refocused distraction from reflections anointed at sleep. Too tired the awakening, too tired the living.

Too tired am I to resurrect my derelict intellect. Banality of evil nothings and murmurings of difference in course. Too tired am I, too tired. Too tired I die.

A Continent of Nations

In preparation for our expedition we letters did write. Pioneering with tales of joy and partings of sorrow, that we might reunite in a different light.

Corps in name and of discovery bound, we knelt up the Missouri we fancied. As we went, we studied all around, earth and god's creatures that were found. By Lou's purchase we travel as we seek a waterway, between a continent of nations, old and new.

Lookout for natives, our excitement drowned, for none were to be found. A president had asked us to ambassador a great gesture, when we meet the Sioux who no one really knew.

On the last eve of August an Eden greats us. Carnivorously we graze on the land, for elk and deer are at hand. The milk of mighty buffalo do replenish us, for next we enter the dangerous bounds.

Maiden natives friendly, until we meet the warring tribe. Nation against nation as events sour, this was not our finest hour. Swords unsheathed as democratic superpower. Now we propaganda menace as to unlock our pilgrims' progress. Unfortunately this is the day, banks of angst are headed our way.

As winter approaches, and without delay camp is forted at Mandan with hay. River turns cold, then to ice, our bodies do chill. Winter lays us still. On lookout for fire tribe, temperature shrinks, as our supplies dwindle, we must rekindle.

Wintering for spring, so our passage may resume, we did write and trade for that is the essence of us Americans. As rains deliver the start again, we dispatch our knowledge home, happy of our progress west.

Now in the wilderness of the caucasian dawning of this land, upstream we venture Rockies bound. June now at river fork, we must separate to search for the way to the great divide, so that our nation we can provide.

Vertical tide of water blocks our path, from our dugouts we must become the portage haulers. Not one, but five great feats we face, carrying our race across the verse.

Winter again now as we abandon the boats. Forlorn we trade for horses and cross the great oats. Higher we climb cold and still, at last we reach where the waters part. Some to the east, some to the west, but all down hill, and that is best.

We descend into madness, as delight at progress and food run fine. We are across the high land and dwindling in the valley of the shadow of our past. At last, the river highway, and soon the great ocean sighted.

Celebrate we do, and jest in the storm of our completion, from east to west. For without ships to take us, we must regress. For how long ago our letters must have been opened, and tears spilt by our bosom friends.

We explorers full of optimism, now dread the pessimism we must endure, as we wait at the foot of our familiar rocky winter beast, the timely barrier, that we must ease.

On journeys return, we may shoot ourselves, but courage abound we will reach our goal, now that to us America is whole. For two years, four months and ten days we did Lewis and Clark on this great lark.

That Moment

You feel it, or you have felt it. That moment when you are not yourself. Free of the shallows you ignore to function. Free of the gay abandonment of joy that distracted you at your focus high.

The moment that you are not yourself, the moment you are a blank slate, free to paint. But how to turn, and rework your old master. How often the same hills, the same animals. What should be new, should you paint it bold?

You drudge familial lines and speak the same meter with the same instruments. That moment when you are not yourself, if only that moment could last.

Searching the New World

From the heights of Khatsahlano's rest at the dawn of day, before the Magee house did wake, I looked out alone over at English bay. I saw the downtown core and its coat of mountain scape, with the big country sky calling pioneer spirit to me, I heard my grandfather whisper, "I made my fortune on this quest out to the west, and now I want you to add to your nest." I looked out and saw from the ephemeral, a commercial pot of honey and I was hungry for success.

I said goodbye to the Magees, who had put me up at my mum's bequest. Into the city that day I found work and a new place to rest. I wondered what Canada could make of me, in a few months I would see. By day I worked and at night I read, but I wanted to get out and discover what I could see, would this land accept me, in my Deuteronomy.

Then one night whilst flicking pages, I saw before me a picture of a spirit bear. I wondered if it was named by the first peoples whose land I now farmed for me. I grew curious and decided to search for the bear, as if it were a part of me.

With friends I travelled along the sunshine coast, settling on an island in the passage. I idled by day and I swam from the beach, out far and beyond the reach. Once I saw an orca pod arise, to my surprise. One eve we feasted on mushrooms and Oscar's greens, and to my delight that night as the floatplane came, I did see a way for me.

I crossed the passage to Lund and continued my quest. I caught a fishing boat to the north and landed at Prince Rupert, an appropriate name for a bear hunt I thought. By a carving shed[1] I met a Tsimshian[2] who regaled with tales of a time in Hartley Bay, where he went fishing for salmon on Gribbell island, only to be chastised by my MacGuffin[3] away.

For months I worked to the bone in a local Inn, on night shifts and slept while tourists' whales were watched. Then after recuperating my funds, I did charter an encounter with a boat to Hartley Bay. There I found a dugout canoe and did paddle too. I arrived on Gribbell late in the day, I had to be quick to make my stay. I portaged my cannon along a salmon run, and arose a hundred feet, to an inland lake where I laid anchor middlemost, and slept with my keep.

Twice more I portaged and slept in my waterside hotel. On the third morning supplies running low, I climbed the peak so I might seek a view to hunt without a punt. There from the eagle's nest I did see, an island within a new lake shining back at me, and on that island are three dark shapes, moving slowly on the shore. Was it to be my bear and me.

I climbed the ridge and a great tree, for there might be bear hunting me. I watched for ages and fell asleep in the heat of the day. With a stark awakening jolt, I did feel the cold of night, as a squawk made me fright. Down the trunk I did skunk, and dalliance the path down to the lake.

I tripped on air and found from the ground my head would not carry me. As I lay there, I wept for what had crept over me. I wondered in strange shapes where the trees spiralled into the stars, and the moon a white bears face did make, and then he did wink at me.

I stumbled into the water with my canoe, and back between the mountain views, I did slumber upon the day. Hence I awoke on the beach with my feet lapped by the water, as my thirst hit me with a different order. I was on Savary Island, and had never left. This filled me with bereft, for it was not to be, I did not see the spirit bear that rested in me. I think of my bear like the hunting of the Snark, and all around me it was still dark.

We hitchhiked our way back to Vancouver. A year had passed to the day, and I must depart as my visa was away. I reached the airport island, and the girl at the desk said "Welcome sir, homeward bound?", and that is what got to me. These changes in my attitude, with this differing longitude reminded me of a time in Key West, with the parrot heads who knew best.

Now coming into ground over brown fields, where there had been England's green and pleasant land. In the memories of an excited youth, all I could think about was the recount by Nairn, of London's grey architecture and bowler hats. I can see him now, leaning out of the number 9 bus without any fuss.

The subway to the city exposed my alien culture, for it had been the Tube when I left. Now opening out on to Piccadilly, the sidewalks not pavements were covered with continental cafés that had arrived in my absence. What was this nuance, this air of grace. Could I slip back between the streets of London. I hummed to Ralph McTell as I walked listening to the city talk. I realised that the quest out west had not been for that pot of honey, but for the bear within me, which I still did not see.

---

[1] "carving shed": A place where first nation artists work on totem poles and carvings discussing stories of their histories.

[2] The Tsimshian are an indigenous people of the Pacific Northwest Coast. Their communities are mostly in coastal British Columbia and far southern Alaska, around Terrace and Prince Rupert in British Columbia, and Alaska's Annette Island.

The Tsimshian people comprise of approximately 10,000 members belonging across seven member First Nation peoples, which include the Kitselas, Kitsumkalum, and the Allied Tribes of the Lax Kw'Alaams, Metlakatla, Kitkatla, Gitga'at (at Hartley Bay) and Kitasoo.

[3] MacGuffin: In fiction, a MacGuffin (sometimes McGuffin or maguffin) is a plot device in the form of some goal, desired object, or other motivator that the protagonist pursues.

About the Author

Benbo Smith was born in London, England in the early 1970s, and is a graduate of the University of Hull. This book is his first fictional work in many years.

Engage with the Author

The author of this work encourages interaction with his audience and will engage with reader feedback and discussion on the work in this publication.

Visit the author's website: BenboSmith.UK

Follow the author on:

Twitter: BenboSmithUK
Facebook: BenboSmithAuthor
Instagram: ProsePoet
YouTube: Benbo Smith

About the Publisher

Splashlime is a small UK independent publishing house based in London. Splashlime believes that we are moving into a new publishing epoch where the printed word and digital reading experience complement each other.

www.ingramcontent.com/pod-product-compliance
Lightning Source LLC
Chambersburg PA
CBHW020624120726
47905CB00003B/935